Angel Jeter

Celebrate Being You

Bumblebee
Books

A CIP catalogue record for this title is
available from the British Library.

ISBN: 978-1-83934-951-5

Bumblebee Books is an imprint of
Olympia Publishers.

First Published in 2024

Bumblebee Books
Tallis House
2 Tallis Street
London
EC4Y 0AB

Printed in Great Britain

www.olympiapublishers.com

Dedication

I dedicate this book to my Grandmother Madeline Jeter, who was strong and independent before it became fashionable..

This book belongs to:

____

In the French Quarter of New Orleans, Louisiana,
lives Marie Laveau.
Marie is a sweet young girl, learning the ways of the world, by
always doing what her mother and grandmother teach her, yet she
is also interested in understanding her ideas about life.
She talks with her mother and grandmother about her thoughts,
creativity, and everything else she questions in her mind.
Marie wants to help people achieve their dreams, but is afraid she
will be bullied, as she is just a child and not strong like an adult.
The grandmother tells her, "Strength is not just in one's body size,
it is in one's mind!"
The mother replies, "I will always be here to help you with anything
you want to achieve until you are strong enough to do it yourself."

Now full of cheer because of the support from her mother and grandmother, Marie steps out to help others. While out in the French Quarter, she meets a young boy named, Andre Cailloux. He is sweet, loving, and carefree. Just like Marie, Andre has great ideas too of how to help other people.
"I want to protect those who can't protect themselves and make sure people all over the world remember my name, but I am just a little kid," says Cailloux.

Marie asks, "How will you protect others until you are strong enough to protect yourself?"

Andre replies, "Since I have not finished becoming a man. I will make sure I tell my mom and dad about bad people, so they can make sure that bad person can't hurt anyone, anymore. I will read and learn as much as possible about the heroes I want to be like. In doing so, I will know one day that people will read about me and want to be strong like me."

As the day goes on Marie Laveau and Andre Cailloux share stories about their families. They don't make each other feel bad about not having the same things at home, instead, they understand that they are different and enjoy being friends.
Marie and Andre decide to go find more kids to help, with the hopes of building a better friendship and making more along the way!

Now at the bayou, they see a young boy named Jules Lion.
Jules is very artistic, he loves to paint, draw, and create beautiful
artwork. Marie and Andre asked Jules, "Why does this
make you so happy?"
Jules said, "Because I love to show people things that they can't
see for themselves, I want to share with the world what I see, like
how your eyes see things and your brain remembers it as if you are
experiencing it for the first time."
Jules continues to tell Marie and Andre that sometimes people
make fun of him because he is not playing sports and that hurts
him for being different.

Being different is the greatest thing in the world, I am different, Andre is different, now we are all friends, and you don't have to feel alone anymore, says Marie!
Andre goes on to tell Jules that drawing and painting is a sport because you must develop visual ideas and it takes a team to support them. So, can I and Marie be on your team? And together you can paint the story of how we all came to know each other and the great things we will do together.

Jules creates a portrait of his new friends. "This artwork will one day let everyone in the world know that they are not alone in making their dreams come true, from children to adults," said Lion! When Jules is finished creating his artwork, he, Andre, and Marie decide to go find someone to show it to. They head back to Marie's house and on the way, they run into a girl named, Jane.

Jane looks very sad and lonely. Marie asks, "Why are you so sad?"
Jane replies, "Because I don't have any family and people make me
feel bad for not having a home."
Andre says, "Would you like to be a part of our family?!"
Jane smiles and says, "Of course!"

Then Jules begins to draw a portrait of the smile his new friend has
on her face. Marie, Andre, Jules, and Jane will spread the message
of happiness, hope, kindness, and love to make the
world a better place!

Marie introduces her new friends to her mother and grandmother, now at Marie's house. She tells them all the great things they can do and how it has helped her and will help others. Marie's mother and grandmother celebrate each of their achievements and encourage them to never forget their dreams. Andre tells his new friends that he would like them to meet his parents, so they leave Marie's house and go to his home.

While walking to the home of Andre Cailloux they come across a boy named, Lafcadio Hearn. Jane asks him, "Why are you by yourself?" Lafcadio says, "Because the people who told me they would be my friends, just lied to me to use my secrets to hurt me."
Jane tells Lafcadio, "I understand, seeing how I didn't have a family until I met Marie Laveau, Andre Cailloux, Jules Lion, and now you, Lafcadio Hearn.

"We all know how it feels to trust someone who is supposed to help you but instead only hurts you," says Marie.
"We're heading to my house to tell my parents about the day we had and the new friends we made. Would you like to come?" Andre asked.
"When we get to Andre's home, we can tell his parents about your problem and they will help you because a good parent knows best and does their best to protect you," says Marie.

The day is late, and the sun has set they arrive at Andre's home and are greeted by his mother and father. Andre's father Gabriel Prosser is a big gentle giant of a man, his mother looks like a Queen, and she is tall and beautiful. Both parents have enchanting smiles. That is one family trait his new friends can see Andre Cailloux inherited. Andre's parents don't want his new friends walking home so late at night, so we all walk home together, and we talk along the way about what we did today and what we will do the next time we get to play again together.

Jane did not have a home,
so she was able to live with Marie Laveau.

Lafcadio told his parents about his problems, and they told him that now he has real friends that won't use his secrets to make him feel bad. It was a good thing he knew to stop hanging out with people who make him feel bad.

Jules Lion was greeted at the door of his home by his family, as he rushed inside to show them the artwork that he created was inspired by his new friends he made today.

Now that everyone was at home safe with their families, Andre walked hand in hand with his mother and father. Andre told his parents, "I am happy I made a positive change today in my new friends' life and they made one in mine, and in return, we all gave each other the greatest reward, "A smile!"

Acknowledgements

I want to thank the city of New Orleans for
all its historical figures, lively music, cultural
education, and delicious food.

Remember, family is not always what you were
born into, it is something you create. Kindness
is always sincere. Thank you for taking the
time to read my book.

Now go out into the world and manifest
your legacy!